Chris Higgins

Illustrated by Lee Wildish

First published in Great Britain in 2015
by Hodder Children's Books

10 9 8 7 6 5 4 3 2 1

A Catalogue record for this book is available from the British Library

ISBN 978 1 444 92575 3

Typeset and designed by Avon DataSet Ltd, Bidford on Avon, Warwickshire

Printed and bound in Great Britain by Clays Ltd, St Ives plc

Hodder Children's Books
a imprint of Hachette Children's Group
Part of Hodder & Stoughton
Carmelite House, 50 Victoria Embankment
London, EC4Y 0DZ
An Hachette UK company

www.hachette.co.uk

For *my* funny family.

Thanks to Vinny for the title.

Chapter 1

'You should have been called Hattie, not Mattie,' says Uncle Vesuvius.

I giggle. I know what he means, I wear hats all the time. I've got billions.

Well, not billions, that would be an exaggeration. But I have got loads.

I've got:

- Woolly hats
- Sun hats
- Floppy hats

- Animal hats
- And my current favourite, a top hat from when we did the talent show.

I'm wearing it now while I sit at the kitchen table, drawing them all.

'You wear one too,' I point out.

'You're right.' Uncle Vesuvius gets to his feet and rubs his back with a groan. 'Only it's always the same one. It's like me, old and battered.'

'You're not old and battered,' I say to be polite. But he is really.

He picks up his own hat. 'I'll be out the back if you want me, Mattie. You alright on your own for a bit?'

'Yep. The others will be home soon.' I choose a green and a yellow felt tip and carefully start to colour in my bobble hat.

I love Uncle Vez (that's what we call him for short). He lives with us now because he'd be on his own otherwise.

We are the Butterfields and there are quite a lot of us. Here is a list of the people in my family. (I like making lists almost as much as I like wearing hats.)

1. Mum
2. Dad
3. Dontie, my brother (twelve years old)
4. Me, Mattie (nine)
5. V, my sister (eight)
6. Stanley, my brother (five)

7. Anika, my sister, who's three (together they are known as Stanika)

8. Will, my baby brother, who's a few months old

9. Jellico, our crazy dog (technically, he's not a person but he's still part of our family)

10. Hiccup, my rabbit (ditto)

11. Uncle Vez (because he lives with us)

12. Grandma and Granddad (because they live close by and are always popping in, especially round tea-time, which drives Mum potty)

I expect you can guess that our house is pretty crowded. Though not as crowded as it used to be because we knocked through into next door and made it twice as big.

Today it's really quiet. Everyone's out except me, plus Hiccup and Uncle Vez in the back garden.

Uncle Vez has been looking after me while I've been off school with an ear infection. I'm nearly better now.

I can't wait to go back to school tomorrow. I bet my best friend Lucinda has really missed me.

I can't wait for the others to come home from school.

I'm bored being on my own.

RAT-A-TAT-TAT!

Hurrah! They're early! I jump to my feet and fling open the front door.

Uncle Vez is standing there, smiling at me with his twinkly eyes.

That's strange. He's not wearing his battered old hat anymore. He's wearing one with corks dangling off it instead.

I thought he was in the back garden. So ...

What's he doing out the front?

Who's that lady with him?

And why is he wearing shorts?

Chapter 2

Uncle Vez opens his mouth to speak and things get even stranger.

'G'day!' he says. 'Now tell me, which one are you? Matisse or Vera-Lynn?'

I stare at him, bewildered. Uncle Vez never calls me by my full name and he knows who I am.

'I'm Mattie!'

'Of course you are, sweetie!' says the lady. 'Love the hat!'

'Good to meet you, Mattie!' says Uncle

Vez and he chuckles deep in his throat.

His chuckle sounds the same as usual but his voice is different. Still cracked and gravelly, but for some reason it's going up at the end of his sentences.

This is very confusing. Then it dawns on me.

'You're not Uncle Vez, are you?'

'Aah, bless you poppet. No, he's not,' says the lady. 'We'd better introduce ourselves. I'm Audrey and this is Norman.'

Her voice is loud and goes up at the end too. Audrey is very large, head and shoulders above Norman. I study her carefully. She has a big bosom, bigger even than Grandma's, and she's wearing a flowery blouse and men's trousers.

The two of them stand there smiling at me.

Norman is so like Uncle Vez, it's unbelievable. Except, now that I'm having a good look, I can see there are differences after all.

Uncle Vez's face is red. Norman's is brown.

Uncle Vez has a ballpoint pen behind his right ear. Norman doesn't.

Uncle Vez has got deep cracks in his face. So has Norman but he's got a big scar as well, above his right eye.

'How did you get that?' I ask, curiously.

'Got kicked in the face by a crazy roo,' he answers in his funny voice that makes everything sound like a question.

I wonder what a crazy roo is.

The lady smiles at me. 'Mattie dear, is Albert at home?'

'Nobody called Albert lives here.'

Norman frowns and scratches his head, just like Uncle Vez does when he's puzzled. 'That's strange. We went to his old address to surprise him and we were told that he'd moved in here with the Butterfields.'

'That's us!' I say and Norman grins.

'Right! Now we're getting somewhere. Tell me Mattie, d'you have an old codger like me living with you who goes by the name of Albert Trot?'

'No,' I say regretfully; I'd like to help. 'The only person like you who lives with us is Uncle Vez.'

'That'll do!' shouts Audrey triumphantly. 'Mattie love, go and tell your Uncle Vez that his long-lost brother from Australia has turned up at his door like a bad penny!'

Chapter 3

When I go out to the shed and tell Uncle Vez that his brother is at the front door he is so surprised that everything stops working.

First his jaw drops open.

Then he lets go of the plant he's repotting and it crashes to the floor.

Then his legs wobble and he sits down heavily on the ground. He looks up at me and opens and closes his mouth like a goldfish but no words come out.

WORRY ALERT!

I rush back to Norman and Audrey.

'Uncle Vez is having a heart attack!'

'Lead the way!' bawls Audrey, rolling up her sleeves. 'I'm trained in CPR!'

But by the time we get out to the shed Uncle Vez is up on his feet again. When he sees Norman his arms and voice come back too.

Uncle Vez flings his arms around his brother, just like Anika does every day when Stanley comes out of school, and hugs him tight like he'll never let him go. Both of them rock to and fro in a weird sort of dance and pat each other on the back, saying, 'Oh Norman,' 'Oh Albert,' over and over again.

After a while Audrey says 'My turn!' and holds out her arms to Uncle Vez, who disappears inside them and loses his voice once more. Then she puts him down and sweeps me up. It's like being hugged by a gigantic, soft squashy cushion that squeezes all the breath out of you but is so comfy you don't ever want it to end.

'What's CPR?' I ask when I've got my breath back.

'Cardiopulmonary resuscitation,' she says, which are the longest words I've heard in my life. 'It's how you rescue someone who's having a heart attack. I'll show you how to do it one day.'

'Cool.' I look at her with respect, then remember my manners. 'Would you like a cup of tea?'

'You're a girl after my own heart, Mattie Butterfield,' says Audrey.

I grin at her happily. I like Audrey. I like Norman too because he's the spitting image of Uncle Vez.

I can't wait for the others to meet them.

Chapter 4

We're having a nice cup of tea and a slice of Grandma's boiled fruit cake, catching up on old times. It turns out that Norman isn't completely long-lost after all. He and Uncle Vez have been in touch on-and-off over the years but they haven't seen each other for a very long time.

'Delicious,' says Audrey, licking the crumbs from her fingers. 'I'll make you one of my pumpkin cakes one day, Mattie.'

'You can't make cake out of pumpkins!' I say in surprise. 'You make Halloween lanterns out of them!'

'Oh yes, you can. Audrey's pumpkin cake is famous!' says Norman. Then we hear the others at the front door and I jump up to let them in.

'Wait, Mattie! Let's surprise them!' says Uncle Vez and he pushes Audrey and Norman into the coat cupboard. 'Quick! Hide!'

Uncle Vez is acting like he's a kid again. On his signal I open the door and Mum, V, Stanley, Anika, baby Will and Jellico spill into the house.

'Nice and quiet in here!' says Mum as everyone dumps their stuff in the hall. 'You're looking better, Mattie. What have you been up to?'

'Nothing!' says Uncle Vez before I can open my mouth. Jellico sniffs around busily, comes to a halt in front of the coat cupboard and starts to bark like crazy.

'Quiet, Jellico!' orders Mum. 'What's got into you? Hang your bags and coats up, everyone.'

From inside the cupboard comes the unmistakeable sound of muffled giggling. Everybody freezes except for Uncle Vez who puts his hands in his pockets and starts whistling. Mum eyes him suspiciously and pulls open the cupboard door.

'SURPRISE!'

Audrey and Norman burst out with their arms in the air, like two jack-in-the-boxes, the corks on Norman's hat bobbing about crazily.

Mum shrieks.

V screams.

Jellico leaps up at them, barking hysterically.

Anika sits down with a thud on her well-padded bottom.

Baby Will chuckles his head off.

'Who are you?' asks Stanley.

'And what are you doing in our coat cupboard?' adds V, who is feeling a bit silly for having screamed out loud.

'Uncle Vez?' Anika stares at Norman, then Uncle Vez, then back at Norman, trying to work out why there's two of him.

Uncle Vez is laughing so much it's left to me to do the introductions. 'This is

Norman and Audrey,' I explain. 'Norman is Uncle Vez's long-lost brother.'

'All the way from Australia,' adds Audrey.

Mum's face lights up. 'I know who you are!' She gives a little jump and claps her hands, just like Anika does when she's excited. 'You're Uncle Bruce and Aunty Sheila!'

Chapter 5

'I don't get it,' says V, frowning. She folds her arms grumpily. V gets very cross if she doesn't understand things properly. 'Who are they? Norman and Audrey, or Uncle Bruce and Aunty Sheila?'

'Norman and Audrey,' says Audrey.

'No, they're not!' insists Mum. 'When I came to live with Uncle Vez and Aunty Etna he told me he had a brother and sister-in-law who lived in Australia and their names were Uncle Bruce and

Aunty Sheila.'

'Sorry Norm!' says Uncle Vez, looking a bit shame-faced. 'She's right. I did.'

'Why?' demands V.

'I don't know. That's what we used to call people who lived Down Under in those days. Bruce or Sheila.'

'It's a nickname, V, like Uncle Vesuvius,' I explain. 'His real name is Albert.'

'Is it?' V stares at Uncle Vez in surprise. 'So why do we call him Uncle Vesuvius?'

'That's my fault.' Now it's Mum's turn to look embarrassed. 'I called him that because he belched and smoked a lot. Like the volcano. Aunty Edna smoked too so I called her Aunty Etna. After another volcano.'

We all pause for a moment to remember Aunty Etna who died.

Audrey breaks the silence by shrieking with laughter. 'Maybe Uncle Bruce and Aunty Sheila aren't so bad after all. You can call us that if you want to.'

'OK.' Everyone stares at them with interest.

'Why do you call Australia *Down Under*?' asks Stanley.

'Because it's the other side of the world,' explains Uncle Bruce in his up-at-the-end voice. I'm going to practise talking like him later. 'It's going on fifty years since I went out there all on my own on a big ship. It took me six weeks to get there.'

'Six weeks?' squeaks V. 'Why did you go all that way?'

'To make my fortune and look for the most beautiful girl in the world,' says Uncle Bruce.

'Did you find her?' asks V.

'I most certainly did.' He smiles at Aunty Sheila.

He means her!

I stare at Aunty Sheila smiling back at him and see that actually, she is beautiful, in a big, bouncy sort of way, like a St Bernard dog. I could imagine her coming across poor little Uncle Bruce, lost and alone in a strange land, and bounding to his rescue.

'Aw, you sentimental old wuss!' booms

Aunty Sheila and we all laugh (even though I'm not sure what a wuss is). 'Time for prezzies, I think. Norman?'

Uncle Bruce nips out to their car obediently and comes back in with a huge bag. Everyone's eyes light up.

But we have to wait for ages because Dontie and Dad come home and it's introductions again, and then we have tea. It's practically bedtime before we finally settle down to open our presents from *Down Under*.

They're worth waiting for though.

They're absolutely brilliant!

Chapter 6

These are the presents that Uncle Bruce and Aunty Sheila brought us from Australia:

Uncle Vez: Australian wild flower seeds

Dad: an aboriginal painting

Mum: opal earrings

Dontie: a didgeridoo

V: a boomerang

Stanley: a giant inflatable crocodile

Anika: a fluffy kookaburra

Will: a cuddly koala bear sleepsuit

Me: a furry kangaroo onesie!

They are all perfect.

I put my onesie on and immediately discover something brilliant. The head is detachable so I can wear it as a hat if I want to!

Uncle Bruce shows Dontie how to play the didgeridoo, which is a very long pipe that you sit on the floor and blow into. It makes a strange noise.

V wants to have a go but Aunty Sheila says she mustn't. Tradition says it's bad luck for girls to play a didgeridoo.

'That's not fair!' protests V.

Aunty Sheila takes V outside and shows her how to throw the boomerang so it comes back to her. V forgets all about the didgeridoo.

Mum loves her dangly opal earrings and Dad is very excited about his painting, a colourful pattern of dots.

Stanley wants to put his inflatable crocodile in the bath so Mum fills it up and there's just enough room to dunk baby Will in beside it. Then she dries him off and dresses him in his new sleepsuit ready for bed. He looks really cute.

Will I mean, not the crocodile.

Aunty Sheila sits on the floor, pulls

Anika onto her lap, and shows her how to press her kookaburra's tummy to make it laugh. Anika makes her do it over and over again.

We're all having a lovely time.

The doorbell rings.

'More visitors?' asks Aunty Sheila.

'It'll be Grandma and Granddad,' I shout. 'I'll get it!'

Chapter 7

I fling open the front door.

'Look what Uncle Bruce and Aunty Sheila brought me!' I say, doing a twirl in my kangaroo onesie.

'Very nice,' says Granddad.

'And me!' says Stanley from behind the giant inflatable crocodile.

'Who are Uncle Bruce and Aunty Sheila?' asks Grandma.

'I got a boomerang. It's my favourite thing ever!' shouts V.

'Look!' squeals Anika, holding up her kookaburra.

'It's like Christmas in here!' laughs Granddad.

'Come and meet them! Uncle Bruce is Uncle Vez's brother!' I say.

'I can see that! Nice to meet you,' says Granddad, shaking Uncle Bruce's hand.

'G'day, mate!'

Anika has climbed onto Aunty Sheila's lap so Aunty Sheila just blows them a kiss.

'Aunty Sheila can do CPR! She's going to teach me how to do it.'

'Well I never!' says Grandma. I don't think she knows what CPR is.

'And she can make pumpkin cake!'

'Fancy that!'

'She's going to make me one!'

'She'll have a job on!' sniffs Grandma.

'No pumpkins around at this time of year.'

'She showed me how to throw my boomerang so it comes back to me. Watch!'

Grandma and Granddad duck just in time as V zooms it over their heads. It crashes into the wall.

'V! What did I tell you? It's not a toy. Now say sorry to your grandparents,' says Aunty Sheila.

'Sorry!' says V meekly.

'Go outside if you want to play with that,' orders Aunty Sheila and V disappears into the back garden. We all stare after her in surprise. Normally she's not that obedient.

'You're good with kids,' remarks Mum.

'Had plenty of practice with our five.

Joelle, Brielle, Narelle, Rochelle and Lorabelle. Right little tearaways. They're all grown up now with kids of their own. None as cute as you though.' She gives Anika a big squashy hug and my little sister snuggles into her happily.

Grandma frowns and holds her arms out towards Anika. 'Come to Grandma,' she says. But Anika is gazing up adoringly at Aunty Sheila.

'More?' she pleads, holding up her kookaburra. Aunty Sheila presses its tummy obligingly and Anika shrieks with laughter.

So does everyone else.

Except Grandma.

Chapter 8

Mum and Dad insist on Uncle Bruce and Aunty Sheila staying with us and before long it feels like they've been here forever.

It's lucky we've knocked through into next door because we've got more room now. We still have to budge up a bit though.

Uncle Vez lets Uncle Bruce bunk in with him. 'Just like old times, Norm,' he says.

'He's like a dog with two tails now he's got his brother back,' says Mum, which

means he's really happy.

Aunty Sheila shares a room with Anika and V comes in with me.

'Nice change not to have to listen to Norm snoring his head off all night long,' says Aunty Sheila.

I like being back with V. When we knocked through I got a bedroom to myself, which is what I always wanted. But sometimes I get a bit lonely or worried and it's nice to have V beside me again.

We lie there giggling at Aunty Sheila snoring through the wall. 'She actually snores louder than Uncle Bruce!' says V. We can hear Uncle Vez and Uncle Bruce chatting away too, and it makes me feel safe.

At school I tell Lucinda all about my Australian aunty and uncle and she tells Mrs Shoutalot, my teacher, who is very interested. She shows us Australia on the globe and now I can see it's true, it really is on the other side of the world.

'No wonder it took Uncle Bruce six weeks to sail there, Miss.'

'Six weeks!' squeaks Tia.

'What's it like there?' asks Alfie.

'It's brilliant. It's got kangaroos and koala bears and kookaburras and crocodiles and sharks.'

'Sharks!' says Alfie, his jaw dropping.

'Crocodiles!' says Joby, his eyes shining.

'What's a kookaburra?' asks Holly.

'It's a bird, a bit like a kingfisher, and it laughs instead of sings.'

'Birds can't laugh!' says Joby scornfully.

'Yes they can, I've heard one!' Though I don't say it wasn't real.

Mrs Shoutalot's eyes light up like they always do when she gets enthusiastic.

'I think we should all find out if kookaburras *can* laugh,' she shouts. 'Everyone sit on the floor quietly and I'll see if I can find a video on the internet.'

We all sit down and wait. And guess what?

Kookaburras really *do* laugh and it's so funny it's catching. We start giggling and before long we're rolling about on the floor howling, and some people are even *crying*, they're laughing so much!

'Ohhh!' Everybody groans in disappointment as the bell goes for playtime.

Mrs Shoutalot wipes her eyes. 'Oh dear,'

she says. It comes out high and squeaky and we all start laughing again.

'Put it back on, Miss!' (Alfie)

'Can we hear it again?' (Lucinda)

'Just one more time?' (this from Joby, who's *never* interested in anything)

'*Please*, Miss!' (most of us)

'More! More! More! More!' (all of us)

Mrs Dunnet, our headteacher, looks through the window to see what is going on. Mrs Shoutalot turns off the computer and shouts, 'That's enough, you lot. Out you go, it's playtime.'

Everyone rushes outside to play Laughing Kookaburras. Except me.

I hang back to talk to Mrs Shoutalot.

'What is it, Mattie?' she sighs, fishing her flask out of her bag. She thinks I'm worried about something but I'm not.

'Please, Miss, I've had an idea.'

'Spit it out then,' she says, pouring herself a cup of coffee.

'I think we should invite Uncle Bruce and Aunty Sheila into school to tell us more about Australia.'

Mrs Shoutalot takes a sip of her coffee, sits back in her chair and studies the ceiling for a long time.

Oh flip! It must have been a bad idea. Now I'm going to get into trouble.

Mrs Shoutalot stops studying the ceiling and looks at me.

'That, Mattie Butterfield, is an excellent idea.'

I run outside to tell all the Laughing Kookaburras in the playground the good news.

Chapter 9

I can't wait to tell Grandma too.

Grandma was on the committee that saved our school from closing down. All the teachers love her because she organized a petition where lots of people signed their name to say they didn't want the school to close. And she was the star of our campaign video.

Grandma loves hearing what we're doing at school.

'Guess what, Grandma!' I say when

she comes round that evening. 'Mrs Shoutalot has invited Aunty Sheila and Uncle Bruce into school to do a talk on Australia.'

I thought she'd be pleased. Instead, she tuts.

'Have you got that outfit on again, Mattie? It's far too warm for that furry old thing.'

Granddad shakes his head, mutters what sounds like, 'Here we go again,' and disappears to the kitchen.

I glance down at my kangaroo onesie in surprise. 'It's not old, Grandma. It's brand new.' But she's not listening.

'Stanley!' she orders. 'Move that crocodile. There are too many people in this house and not enough chairs.'

Stanley grabs his crocodile and scuttles

after Granddad. Anika chases after him.

'Plenty of room over here, Marje,' invites Aunty Sheila, patting the chair beside her.

'No thank you!' says Grandma, her nose in the air, and she squashes in beside Dontie who's playing the didgeridoo.

She puts her fingers in her ears. 'Ooh, what a dreadful noise!' she says rudely. 'It's going right through me!'

'I've got to practise!' says Dontie in a huff, and he stomps out too.

Grandma frowns at V. V frowns at Grandma and leaves the room without a word.

Aunty Sheila stares at Grandma in surprise. Grandma glares back at her, eyes narrowed, legs wide, hands on her knees. Suddenly I think of the boxing Granddad was watching on TV the other day. She's like the existing champion, eyeballing her opponent from the other side of the ring.

I follow V out to the kitchen, leaving Grandma and Aunty Sheila on their own in the lounge.

Everyone else is sitting round the kitchen table.

'Grandma's really grumpy,' I say sadly, sliding in beside them.

Granddad snorts. 'You're telling me. She's like a bear with a sore head.'

'Mad as a cut snake,' sympathises Uncle Bruce.

'Moody as a maggot,' says Granddad.

'Mean as a meat-axe,' adds Uncle Bruce.

'Moany as mud,' says Granddad.

But nobody laughs.

I'm not sure we should be talking about Grandma like that.

'She's not like this normally,' I explain to Uncle Bruce.

'You're right, Mattie, she's not,' agrees Granddad. 'I don't know what's got into her.' He shakes his head and sighs again.

Mum and Dad do that thing where they glance at each other and raise their eyebrows.

Uh oh! They know what it is but they're not saying.

WORRY ALERT!

What's wrong with Grandma?

Chapter 10

Aunty Sheila wears her best flowery dress and high heels when she comes into school.

Uncle Bruce wears shorts, a crocodile T-shirt and his special hat with corks on it.

Everyone wants to try it on. He chooses Holly and it comes right down over her nose.

'What are the corks for?' asks Mad Marcus.

'To keep the flies away,' explains Uncle Bruce.

'What's the deadliest animal in Australia?' asks Eli.

'Good question,' says Uncle Bruce and launches into the answer in great detail.

He talks about saltwater crocodiles that drown you first, then crunch you to pieces with their sharp teeth.

He talks about a snake with enough venom to kill a hundred humans.

He talks about spiders whose bites can kill you in a couple of hours.

He talks about jellyfish
whose stings can kill you
in a couple of minutes.

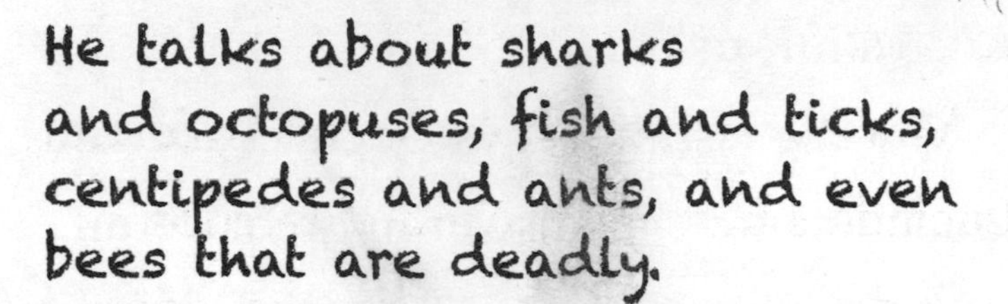

He talks about sharks
and octopuses, fish and ticks,
centipedes and ants, and even
bees that are deadly.

'Bees can't kill you!' says Lewis scornfully.

'They can in Australia,' says Uncle Bruce.

Everybody listens open-mouthed. It's never been this quiet in my classroom before.

When he finally stops, no one says a word.

Then Lucinda says, in a quiet little voice not a bit like her normal loud, confident one, 'I don't think I want to go to Australia. It's scary.'

Mrs Shoutalot looks a bit worried. Lucinda's mum is a school governor.

'*I* do!' says Eli, but even he doesn't sound quite so sure anymore.

'Aw, don't listen to him, you never ever get to see those critters,' booms Aunty Sheila. 'They might be capable of killing you, but they never do. They're more scared of you than you are of them.'

Then she shows us slides of kangaroos in her top paddock and lorikeets in her kitchen garden. Lorikeets are pretty, brightly-coloured parrots but Aunty Sheila says they're pests because they damage the crops.

'How big is your farm?' asks Eddy, who lives on one himself.

'About a thousand hectares.'

'How big's a hectare?' persists Joby, who normally hates maths.

'About the size of a rugby field,' says Aunty Sheila and everyone gasps. A thousand rugby fields!

'That's one big farm,' says Eddy with respect.

'Tell us about the kangaroos,' pleads Mad Marcus.

So she does.

Here are some interesting facts about kangaroos.

They can hop at about 65 kilometres an hour, which is faster than Granddad drives.

- The males can grow to about three metres – that's even taller than Mr McGibbon, Stanley's teacher, who's the tallest man we know.

- Their babies are called joeys and the mum can choose to have a boy or a girl. (I *think* that's true.) Lucinda said she'd have two boys and two girls and Alfie said he'd have all boys if kangaroo girls were as annoying as Lucinda.

- The joeys are born very early and they have to stay in their mum's pouch for months and months until they can survive on their own. (A pouch is like a furry pocket on their mum's tummy.)

Most amazing of all, when times are hard, like if there's a drought or something, the pregnant mums can hold off giving birth until things get better.

'What a brilliant idea!' shouts Mrs Shoutalot, getting excited. 'If I was a kangaroo I'd wait till my mortgage was paid off.'

'Sshhh!' we say, because this is interesting.

'Sorry!' she says and quietens down while Aunty Sheila goes on to talk about animals we've never heard of before. Like possums and wombats and quokkas and quolls.

'Lots of them come out at night so

they're called nocturnal animals,' she explains.

'What do you call an animal that comes out during the day?' asks Lucinda, which sounds like a joke.

But it's not because Aunty Sheila says, 'Diurnal.'

'I'm going to tell my mum that!' says Lucinda and Mrs Shoutalot beams.

Aunty Sheila shows us a photo of a creature called a bilby. It's like a cross between a rabbit and a mouse and it's really cute.

'I wish I could go to Australia to see one for myself,' I say longingly.

'Do you, darling?' Aunty Sheila smiles at me and I smile back at her. This is so interesting. When the bell goes for the end of school, nobody wants to go home.

'Thank you!' says Mrs Shoutalot. 'The children loved it and they've learned so much!'

Everyone choruses, 'Thank you!' to our visitors and gives them a huge clap. I feel very proud of my Australian aunty and uncle.

Especially when Mrs Shoutalot adds, 'You should have been a teacher, Mrs Trot!'

Chapter 11

After school everyone gathers around Uncle Bruce and Aunty Sheila in the playground. They're like celebrities! Everybody wants to try on Uncle Bruce's hat. It takes ages.

Naughty George from Stanley's class won't take it off. He runs away with it on and

Mr McGibbon has to chase after him.

'It's not fair!' says V when we're finally walking home. This is something she says a lot. 'Can't you come and talk to our class too?'

'And mine!' says Stanley. He's hop-skipping along beside us, pretending to be a kangaroo.

'One day,' says Aunty Sheila. 'Tell you what? How about we make you an authentic Aussie tea tonight?'

Everyone perks up.

'What are we having?' asks V.

'Bush tucker.'

'What's bush tucker?' asks Stanley who likes collecting new words and phrases.

'Ah, just roo ... or croc ... or witchetty grub ...'

We stare at Uncle Bruce, wide-eyed.

Roo is kangaroo. Croc is crocodile. Witchetty grub is … I don't know, but I don't like the sound of it.

'I'm vegetarian!' I say quickly, which is the truth.

'Me too!' say V and Stanley, which is a fib.

Uncle Bruce isn't listening. He marches into Kumar's, our corner shop, and we all trail in after him.

'Good afternoon. Do you have any kangaroo, crocodile or witchetty grubs today?' he asks.

Mr Kumar shakes his head regretfully. 'We're completely out of them, I'm afraid. We've got fish fingers if they're any good.'

V, Stanley and I breathe a big sigh of relief but Uncle Vez shakes his head.

'I'll take six packs of your finest snags instead.'

My heart sinks as Mr Kumar picks six packets of sausages out of the fridge. I haven't eaten meat since I went on holiday to Sunset Farm last summer and discovered that beef came from cows, and pork came from pigs, and lamb came from real lambs, and chicken was real chickens.

'Don't forget veggie snags for our Mattie,' says Aunty Sheila and I brighten up.

'Don't suppose you've got any yabbies?' asks Uncle Bruce hopefully.

Mr Kumar sighs sadly and holds up empty hands. 'I am very sorry. I'm afraid we're out of those too.'

'No worries, mate. Just chuck in a big

bag of prawns for the barbie,' says Uncle Vez.

Everyone's face lights up.

Me: 'Are we having a barbecue?'

Stanley: 'What are yabbies?'

V: 'What's for afters?'

'I'll take some flour, sugar, a few apples and maple syrup while you're at it,' Aunty Sheila instructs Mr Kumar.

Me: 'What for?"

'Chuck in a few tinnies too,' adds Uncle Bruce.

Stan: 'What are tinnies?'

I have noticed two interesting things about Uncle Bruce and Auntie Sheila.

1. They don't always answer your questions. This may be because:

A. They are old

B. They are deaf

C. They are not listening

D. They are Australian

2. Although they speak the same language as us (English), they have extra words and sayings that we don't have.

I mention this to Aunty Sheila and she says, 'That's good. We're extending your vocabulary.'

'How come you speak Australian, Mr Kumar?' asks V.

'I watch *Neighbours*,' he explains. Then he adds, 'And my brother has a restaurant in Sydney.'

Mr Kumar always answers questions properly.

When we get home Uncle Vez and Uncle Bruce make a barbecue in the back garden out of stones and sticks and charcoal.

'Yippee! No cooking for me tonight!' says Mum, bouncing baby Will up and down in her arms. He gives a big, gummy laugh and Jellico barks excitedly.

'It's like Bonfire Night!' says Stan.

The fire has to burn down before we can put the snags on it. While we're waiting, Stanley and I go inside and start making a list of Australian words and meanings that we've learnt so far. We make a good team because Stanley likes collecting new words and I like making lists.

Anika comes too because she's never very far from Stan. It's nice sitting at the kitchen table with Aunty Sheila busy at the stove making something out of the flour and sugar and apples and maple syrup she'd bought from Mr Kumar.

She helps us with the meanings if we get stuck.

That's what we're doing when Grandma and Granddad arrive.

Chapter 12

'Grandma! Listen! We're making an Australian phrasebook. This is what we've got so far!'

Stanley is good with words. He won a prize for reading and Grandma was very proud. I read out the Australian word and he gives the English meanings.

ME:	STANLEY:
G'day	hello
wuss	big softie
paddock	big field

witchetty grubs	white, caterpillar-type grubs that you can **eat alive** (though you probably wouldn't want to)
grub	food (not to be confused with a witchetty grub)
nosh	another word for food
tucker	**ANOTHER** word for food (Australians like their food. I do too)
bush tucker	wild food off the land
roo	kangaroo
croc	crocodile
snags	sausages
tinny	a can of beer
bilby	a rabbit/mouse-like creature
diurnal	daily. I think we have this word in English too
possums, wombats, quokkas and quolls	more Australian creatures
yabbies	a **BIG** prawn that lives in a dam
dam	a pond on an Australian farm (not the same as dams in this country)

'Well, I never!' says Granddad, chuckling.

Grandma sniffs. 'So, we're speaking Australian now, are we? We'll all be singing *Waltzing Matilda* next.'

'Who's *Waltzing Matilda*?' asks Stanley but Grandma must have caught the no-answering bug because she doesn't reply.

'Aunty Sheila's helping us extend our vocabulary,' I explain. 'She gave a talk at our school today and Mrs Shoutalot said she should have been a teacher!'

'Did she now?' Grandma sounds unimpressed.

That's funny. I thought Grandma was a big fan of education. I'm sure Dad said she would have liked to have been a teacher herself.

'Snags are ready!' bawls Uncle Bruce

from the back garden. 'Come and get them!'

We all rush out except for Aunty Sheila who's still at the stove and Grandma who looks as if she can't decide whether to stay in the kitchen or come outside with us.

In the end she follows us outside.

Chapter 13

It's fun standing around the fire, especially when it gets dark and the moon comes up. We eat burnt snags smothered in onions and tomato ketchup, in bread rolls dripping with melted butter. Delicious.

'It's like being on holiday in Cornwall,' says V, and it is.

'Maybe one day we could go on holiday to Australia,' I say hopefully.

Grandma sniffs.

'Here, Albert. Catch.' Uncle Bruce

chucks Uncle Vez a can of beer. 'Arnold? Wanna crack open a tinny?'

'Don't mind if I do, Norm,' says Granddad and the funny thing is he sounds almost as Aussie as Uncle Bruce.

Grandma sniffs again and rolls her eyes.

When Dad and Dontie come home they join us in the back garden. It's quite crowded with all of us and our statues.

'Where did these come from?' asks Uncle Bruce.

'Dad made them,' I say proudly. 'Every time someone has a birthday in our family he makes them a statue. That's Will's seal.'

'They're pretty impressive. D'you sell them, Tim?'

'No, they're just for family,' explains Dad.

'Lucky family,' says Uncle Bruce. 'They're really good.'

Dad has a tinny and Dontie wants one too but Uncle Bruce says he's not allowed because he's just an ankle-biter.

'What's an ankle-biter?' asks Dontie.

'A kid,' says Uncle Bruce and everyone laughs, even Dontie. I make a mental note to add *ankle-biter* to my Australian phrasebook.

Actually, Grandma doesn't laugh. She sniffs instead, a really long one this time.

'You've got a bad cold, Grandma,' I say sympathetically, and pull my hanky out of my pocket. 'You can use this if you want.'

The grown-ups do that giggling/spluttering/changing-into-a-cough thing, like someone's said the wrong thing, even though nobody has.

'No, thank you,' she says stiffly. 'I think it's time we went home, Arnold.'

But at that moment, Aunty Sheila opens the door and shouts, 'Ta-dah!' with a big smile and one hand in the air. The other is balancing a tray piled high with something that smells **amazing**.

Chapter 14

I've got another word for my Australian words and phrases list.

Damper.

Damper is the best thing I've ever tasted in my life.

Do you know what it is? It's bread that Australian bushmen cook in the ashes of an open fire. It's just flour and salt and water, that's all.

But Aunty Sheila's damper is special. She's wrapped it around slices of apple and smothered it in maple syrup and baked it in the oven. We eat it piping hot.

'Gorgeous!' I sigh, when it's all gone.

'Finger-licking good!' says Granddad and licks his fingers to prove it.

'Delish!' says V.

'Very tasty!' says Dad.

'Sweet,' says Dontie.

'Scrumptious!' says Stan.

'Very more-ish!' says Mum.

'More?' echoes Anika, hopefully.

'Woof!' agrees Jellico, licking his lips.

Everyone looks at Grandma. There is a long pause.

'Very nice,' she says finally in a tight little voice and everybody smiles. Then she adds, 'Although, personally, I'm more partial to pancakes myself.'

Beside me I hear Mum give a little groan.

'Aw no, Marje! I have to disagree with you there,' says Aunty Sheila in her big, loud voice. 'Damper beats pancakes hands down.'

'Surely,' says Grandma, her voice as sweet as maple syrup, 'it depends on how well you make them?'

'Nah, I'm not convinced,' says Aunty Sheila. 'What about you guys?'

We stare first at Aunty Sheila, then at Grandma, then back at Aunty Sheila again.

Next to me Granddad swallows so hard I can actually hear him.

'What do you think, Mattie?' prompts Aunty Sheila.

Oh no! Everyone's eyes are on me.

'Mattie loves my pancakes, don't you darling?' says Grandma.

I do. I love pancakes, anyone's pancakes, I'm not fussy. But damper is delicious too.

I look up at Mum for help. She gives me a tiny shake of her head.

Jellico flops down with his head on his paws and whines deep in his throat.

Grandma draws herself up to her full height.

'Right then,' she announces. 'The proof of the pudding is in the eating. *I* am going to make you all pancakes and then we can put them to the test.'

We watch as Grandma walks straight-backed into the house.

'Pistols at dawn,' chuckles Uncle Vez.

Granddad lets out a deep sigh. 'Chuck

us another tinny, Norm. We could be in for the long haul here.'

Chapter 15

Surprisingly, it doesn't take Grandma that long to whip up a mountain of pancakes.

'Come and get it!' she shouts, and we all troop into the kitchen.

Actually, six mountains of pancakes. I have never seen so many in my life.

'She never does anything by halves,' says Granddad, shaking his head.

'She's emptied my cupboards!' gasps Mum. 'There's nothing left for packed lunches!'

Tonight Grandma has made:

1. Pancakes with lemon and sugar

2. Pancakes with banana and honey

3. Pancakes with strawberry jam and coconut

4. Pancakes with peanut butter and chocolate

5. Pancakes with blueberries and raspberries

6. Pancakes with tinned peaches and yoghurt

'Do have a crêpe,' says Grandma sweetly, wafting them under Aunty Sheila's nose.

FLOUR
FLOUR
FLOUR
ONEY

'The blueberry and raspberry are low calorie.'

'I hid those berries at the back of the fridge for my breakfast!' mutters Mum through gritted teeth.

'Don't mind if I do, Marje,' says Aunty Sheila, helping herself to a banana and honey, and a peanut butter and chocolate as well.

'I thought pancakes only came with lemon and sugar?' I say, puzzled, and grab a peanut butter and chocolate before Aunty Sheila polishes them all off.

'Yummy-yummy-yum-yum.' Anika munches her way stolidly through the plate of jam and coconut while Dad samples the tinned peaches.

'What's a crêpe, Grandma?' asks Stan, his mouth full of blueberries.

'It's the French for pancakes,' says Grandma. 'I'm so sorry, Audrey,' she adds. 'The blueberry and raspberry are rather nice with fromage frais but I'm afraid Mona is out of it. She's out of serviettes too.'

Mum chokes on her peanut butter and Dad thumps her on the back.

'What's fromage frais?' asks Stan. Grandma opens her mouth to answer and then closes it again.

'She doesn't know,' mutters Mum darkly. 'She's just looked up the recipe in my cook book.'

'Why is she speaking French?' asks Dontie.

'Why is she sounding like the Queen?' asks V.

'Who knows?' says Granddad wearily.

'That woman is a mystery to me.' He takes a bite of lemon and sugar and cheers up. 'Tell you one thing, though. She's a great cook.'

Granddad's right. All the pancakes disappear rapidly even though we're already stuffed full of damper.

This is how many I eat:

- Two peanut butter and chocolate (scrummy)
- One lemon and sugar (nice)
- One banana and honey (very sweet)
- Two blueberries and raspberries (I ate one,

then remembered Mum wanted the berries for her breakfast so I took another, picked all the berries off for her, put them in my pocket and ate the pancake on its own)

- Half a jam and coconut (the other half dropped on the ground and Jellico gulped it down before I could pick it up. Boo!)

- A quarter of peaches and yoghurt (messy. V couldn't finish it so I did. Sorry, Jellico)

Chapter 16

'So? What's your verdict?' asks Grandma when all the pancakes have gone.

'Delicious,' says Uncle Vez and gives a little belch. 'Pardon me!'

'Very nice. I'm full as a goog,' says Uncle Bruce, patting his stomach. He's got bits of pancake in his whiskers.

'What's a goog?' asks Stan.

'Some say it's an egg. Others say it's a tick,' explains Aunty Sheila.

'What's a ti—?'

'The point *is*, which one did you like best?' interrupts Grandma.

Everyone starts shouting out their favourite.

'Banana and honey.'

'Chocolate!'

'Jam!'

'You can't beat lemon and sugar!'

'Chocolate!'

'No, I don't mean that!' Grandma holds her hand up and we all fall silent. 'Do you prefer *damper* … (she makes it sound like a bad smell rather than something mouth-wateringly good) … or *my* delicious pancakes?'

Aunty Sheila's mouth twitches like she's going to smile but instead she folds her arms and waits.

Uncle Bruce does that thing that Uncle

Vez does. He puts his hands in his pockets and whistles a tuneless tune.

Stanley's face wrinkles up with concentration. At last he says, 'Pancakes,' and Grandma looks triumphant.

V: 'Damper! With maple syrup.'

Grandma's face falls.

Anika: 'Pancakes.'

Grandma brightens up again even though we all know Anika is just copying Stan.

V (insistent): 'No way! Damper!'

Grandma: 'Dontie? What do you think?'

Dontie: 'Damper.'

Grandma's face falls further.

Stanley: 'Pancakes!'

'Damper!' shouts V.

Dad puts his hand over her mouth like a gag.

'Not an easy decision to make,' he says firmly. 'I think the jury's out on this one.'

'Time for bed!' trills Mum. 'School in the morning!'

'It'll be time for brekkie soon!' agrees Aunty Sheila.

'Can you make us damper for breakfast, Aunty Sheila?' asks V, wriggling free of Dad's hand.

Grandma's face practically hits the ground.

'Bed!' repeats Mum.

That reminds me. I fish the berries out of my pocket and put them in Mum's hands. They're a bit squashed.

'I saved these for you, Mum. For your breakfast muesli. Because you said Grandma had used them all up.'

Mum goes a bit pink. 'Thank you, Mattie,' she says and picks the fluff off them.

Grandma goes pink too. 'Sorry, Mona.'

'That's all right!' lies Mum. 'I don't mind.'

'Come on, Marjorie,' says Granddad gently. 'Time for us to be off.'

He helps Grandma on with her coat and then links his arm through hers. Dad and Mum and I wave them off at the door.

Dad shakes his head as we watch them go. 'My mother is a force to be reckoned with, all right.'

'What do you mean?' I ask.

'He means that Grandma's always busy and on the go,' says Mum, hurriedly.

'I mean that she likes being in charge,'

explains Dad. He and Mum grin at each other.

I know what they really mean. She's bossy.

So what? Someone has to be. She's the Boss of the Butterfield Family. She's the one who gets things done.

These are some of the things she's done over the past few months:

- She helped us with the vegetable patch
- She cooked our Christmas dinner for us
- She sorted out glasses for V
- She found our missing lottery ticket

- She did the costumes for the talent show
- She helped us save our school

But tonight, as I watch her disappear down the road on Granddad's arm, she doesn't look like the Butterfield Family Boss at all.

She just looks old.

Chapter 17

Worry! Worry! Worry!

I punch my pillow hard, three times.

I can't sleep. My worry voice won't let me.

I can't stop thinking about Grandma.

She's getting old. You saw it tonight with your own eyes.

So? What's grey hair and a few wrinkles?

I mean walking-slowly, hanging-onto Granddad's-arm old. Don't pretend you didn't notice.

Don't be daft. Grandma's the Boss. She's always there for us.

Yeah, she is. But she's not going to be around forever. She's getting old.

AAAGH!

Beside me V is flat out and snoring. I wind myself round her and try to breathe in-out, in-out, in time with her snores but I still can't sleep. The mean little voice won't let me.

When people get old like that, all tired and frail, they get sick.

Like Aunty Etna?

I jump up and go into Mum's and

Dad's bedroom. I stand by their bed and wait. Dad is snoring like V only ten times louder but after a while Mum turns over like I knew she would and opens one eye.

'What is it Mattie?' she says wearily.

'Mum? Is Grandma going to die?'

'Not tonight,' she groans and holds the duvet up so I can crawl in. 'What's

brought this on?'

I snuggle in beside her. The bed is nice and warm and smells of Mum and Dad. I feel better already.

'She looked sick and tired tonight when she went home. I'm worried. I think she might be dying.'

Mum snorts. 'She's sick and tired all right, but not the way you mean. Sick and tired of Aunty Sheila getting all the attention, more like.'

I feel all the tension draining away from me. 'What do you mean?'

Mum sighs. 'Remember when V got cross with Stanley for winning the reading prize in assembly?'

'And she tore up his book and got into trouble?'

'Yes. She did it because she was jealous

of him. Well, Grandma's been a bit like that ever since Aunty Sheila arrived.'

I stare into the darkness, trying to understand.

'Grandma is jealous of Aunty Sheila?'

'In a way. She's had her nose put out of joint.'

I think of Grandma with her nose out of joint and giggle.

'She didn't like it when V and Dontie said they liked Aunty Sheila's damper better than her pancakes,' explains Mum.

'But …' I struggle to puzzle it out. 'If we love Aunty Sheila's damper more than Grandma's pancakes it doesn't mean that we love Aunty Sheila more than Grandma.'

'*I* know that! Tell it to Grandma.'

'I will.' I snuggle down happily. Then

I pop my head up again. 'But I still don't get it. I mean, V was only seven then but Grandma's too old to be jealous.'

'We're all seven inside,' says Mum. 'Now go to sleep.'

My mum is the wisest person I know. I snuggle down beside her and feel myself drifting off. And I don't even have to try to match my breathing to hers.

It just comes automatically.

Chapter 18

The next day is Saturday. It's breakfast time and I'm wearing my kangaroo onesie. Dad is doing something mysterious in the shed so we're banned from going out there.

'What are we doing today, Mum?' asks Stanley.

'I think we'll have a nice quiet day,' says Mum.

'Bor-ing!' says V.

The doorbell rings. It's Lucinda with

her mum.

'Haven't seen you for a while,' trills Mrs Packham-Wells, who saw us yesterday. 'Thought we'd pop in and say hello on our way to dance class.'

'Cup of coffee?' asks Mum.

'Don't mind if I do!' says Mrs Packham-Wells, sailing in. 'Are your visitors still here?'

'In the kitchen,' says Mum.

Next appears Rupert Rumble, Stanley's friend, with his mum.

'Just passing!' says Mrs Rumble.

'Coffee?' asks Mum.

'Go on then!' says Mrs Rumble, making straight for the kitchen. 'Hello Mrs Trot, I've heard all about you! Rupert was so disappointed you couldn't speak to his class. He's been dying to meet you!'

The doorbell rings again. 'I'll get it!' I say.

It's Lily Pickles who's allowed out on her own.

'V!' I shout. 'Lily Pickles wants to know if you're coming out to play.'

'No, I don't,' says Lily. 'I want to come in and see Uncle Bruce and Aunty Sheila. Did you know Eddy and Eli are hanging about outside?'

'Come on in, everyone!' beams V. 'It's not a boring day after all.'

'We're really popular today,' I say in surprise.

'Well, somebody is,' says Mum, as everyone gathers around Uncle Bruce and Aunty Sheila. 'Their fame has spread. Who's that peering in at our gate?'

Oh no! It's Mad Marcus from my class

with his big sister, Matilda.

'Sorry,' says Matilda, looking a bit embarrassed. 'Is this where the Australians live? Only our Marcus hasn't stopped going on about them since they came into school. He's got more questions he wants to ask them.'

'We'd better move into the living room,' says Mum. 'Mattie, you may as well leave that door wide open.'

Before long word's got round and more and more kids from school arrive. Dontie stands at the front door and makes them form an orderly queue that stretches down the front path and onto the street. Grandma and Granddad have to push past them to get into the house.

'That's all we need,' mutters Mum when she sees them.

'What's going on here?' asks Granddad.

'Everybody wants to meet our Australian visitors,' I explain.

'It's getting a bit crowded,' says Mum,

looking a bit overwhelmed. 'I'd offer you a cup of tea but there are no cups left. At least our Dontie's doing a good job of keeping them under control.'

'Your Dontie's charging them all 50p to come in!' points out Granddad. 'He's making a bomb!'

'Is he really!' gasps Mum. 'Did you pay?'

'Did I heck!' says Granddad.

'Blooming Aussie celebrities,' growls Grandma.

Mum winks at me and I remember last night and glance up at Grandma. She looks old and cranky when she frowns. When she's jealous.

I fling my arms around her and automatically she hugs me back, just as she always does.

'I love Aunty Sheila's damper, Grandma,' I say solemnly, gazing up at her, 'and I love your pancakes too. But most of all, I love you.'

Her arms tighten around me and her face softens.

'I love you too, Mattie,' she says and she looks happy and normal again.

Chapter 19

More kids keep pouring through the door to speak to Uncle Bruce and Aunty Sheila.

Some of them get bored with waiting.

Mad Marcus starts chasing Jellico around. Jellico is barking like crazy.

Lucinda jumps up on the sofa to get away from him. Other kids copy her and start bouncing up and down on it like a trampoline.

Granddad clears his throat. 'It's

standing room only in here, Marjorie. Shall we leave them to it?'

'Don't go,' says Mum. We all stare at her in surprise.

That's funny. I mean, I know Mum loves Grandma but she usually breathes a sigh of relief when she goes home. Once, when they'd had words, she said she was glad to see the back of her. I'm not sure she's always glad to see the front.

Personally, I love seeing Grandma every day. She's like bread and jam to me. But I think Mum wishes she was more of a treat for special occasions. Like birthday cake.

It's getting very noisy and silly in here. We need Mrs Dunnet to keep control.

My rabbit, Hiccup, has fled up the chimney to hide.

Joby and Alfie are trying to climb up and rescue him and lots of people are egging them on.

WORRY ALERT!

Maybe I should go and get my dad from the shed. Even Aunty Sheila looks like she doesn't know what to do.

'Please stay!' pleads Mum, clutching Grandma's arm. She sounds desperate. 'I need you to sort this lot out.'

Grandma's face lights up. 'No problem.' She holds out an arm and grabs Mad Marcus as he dashes past. 'Not so fast, young man.'

Then she takes a deep breath and roars,

'FREEEEEEEEEEEEEZE!!!'

Everyone stops yelling and stands still.

'SIT!' she orders and dumps Mad Marcus on the floor to illustrate what she means.

Everyone drops down obediently on the spot, including the grown-ups. Joby, Alfie and Hiccup come down from the chimney.

'Dontie, the house is now full to the brim,' Grandma announces. 'No more are allowed in.'

'Health and safety,' agrees Uncle Vez, who was in charge of it at our talent show.

Dontie closes the front door. His pockets are bulging with 50p coins. We hear groans of disappointment from outside.

'Now,' Grandma addresses us all, 'if you want to ask our Australian visitors a question, raise your hand. '

A forest of hands shoots up.

'Listen carefully. *I* will choose who can ask a question and you will all get a turn so long as you sit quietly,' says Grandma sternly. 'Anyone who gets up or shouts out will be asked to leave.'

Everyone sits as still as a statue, with nice straight backs and closed lips. You could hear a pin drop if you had one.

'Stanley, you may go first.'

Stanley asks his question and Uncle Bruce answers it. Grandma points to the next person and so it continues.

'Rupert?'

'Eli?'

'Mrs Rumble?'

'Joby, your turn.'

It's all going really well now Grandma's

in charge. She's parked herself down on the floor between Mad Marcus and Eddy, to keep an eye on them. They're listening really well.

'She should've been a teacher,' I whisper to V.

'No, she should've been a headteacher,' V whispers back.

Grandma looks up. She's heard us.

'Uh oh!' I say. 'Now we're for it.'

But it's OK. She looks pleased.

Chapter 20

This is the best day ever.

We all get to ask a question so we learn loads more about Australia.

At the end, Lucinda sighs longingly. 'It sounds really cool. Can we go there one day, Mum?'

Lucinda's mum laughs. 'There's nothing I'd like more. But it's too expensive, I'm afraid.'

Everyone gasps. It must be a lot of money if the Packham-Wells family can't afford it.

Nobody wants to go home so Uncle Bruce demonstrates how to play the didgeridoo. Then, of course, everybody wants a go.

Grandma makes them line up and Dontie tries to charge them because it's his didgeridoo but Aunty Sheila says it's free.

Dontie sulks.

One by one everyone tries to make a noise on the didgeridoo. It's harder than it looks.

Dad comes in from the shed and has a shock to see so many people crowded into his living room.

Still nobody wants to leave, not even Lucinda who's supposed to be at dance class. Dad has a brainwave.

'Let's go to the park and have a cricket match.'

Dontie perks up. 'Like the Ashes, you mean?'

'What are the Ashes?'

'A series of cricket matches between England and Australia.'

'Uncle Bruce can be captain of Australia and Uncle Vez can be captain of England!' suggests Granddad and they both look very happy about this.

'Um, technically, only Aunty Sheila can play for Australia,' Dontie points out.

'Fair point,' says Uncle Bruce and has a think. 'Just for once we'll allow English people to play for Australia as well. Come on.'

Everyone cheers and rushes off to the park. When we get there we choose an umpire to referee the match (Grandma, naturally), then Uncle Bruce and Uncle Vez take it in turn to pick teams.

I get to play for England.

Lucinda gets to play for Australia.

'Mattie!' she whispers to me urgently. 'I don't know how to play cricket.'

I stare at her in surprise. I thought Lucinda knew everything.

'It's easy! You just hit the ball with the bat and run as fast as you can between the two posts. The team that makes the most runs wins.'

'Like rounders?'

'Sort of. But run straight, not in a circle.'

Australia wins the coin toss and bats first. Soon a big crowd has assembled to cheer us on. It's brilliant fun. Some people are good like Uncle Bruce who makes 34 runs and Dontie who makes 27. Some people don't make any. Like Lucinda.

By the time they are all out, Australia have made 138 runs. Now it's our turn.

Uncle Vez bats first and he makes 20 runs. I bat next and I make three before Dontie catches me out (that's three more than Lucinda). Eddy makes eight, Joby six. But the star of the show is Granddad. He scores a hundred not out, all on his own. This is what's known as a century and everyone cheers and claps him, even Australia.

I'm soooo proud of my granddad. So is Grandma. She gives him a big kiss and Alfie makes sick noises.

Then Granddad scores another two runs and it's all over, because now

England have made 139 so they've beaten Australia even though only five people have had a chance to bat. Australia groans.

'That's not fair!' complains Mad Marcus. 'I didn't even get to have a go.'

'Rules is rules,' says Grandma sternly and Mad Marcus shuts up.

At last, people start drifting off home for lunch.

'Thanks for a great morning,' says Eddy.

'It's been awesome,' says Joby.

'Can we do it again next Saturday?' asks Mad Marcus.

'Aw mate, we'll be long gone by then,' says Uncle Bruce.

My family stare at him, open-mouthed as everyone groans in disappointment.

'Where are you going?' asks Stanley in a tight little voice. Anika slips her hand into his.

'Home, hon,' says Aunty Sheila.

'Home to Australia?' asks V, sounding strangled.

'Afraid so,' says Aunty Sheila, putting her arm around her. 'All good things must come to an end.'

V shakes off Aunty Sheila's hug and stamps her foot. 'Why?' she demands crossly. 'Why must they come to an end? We don't want you to go.'

And then she bursts into tears.

Chapter 21

I've changed my mind. This is the worst day. Ever.

We are upset that Uncle Bruce and Aunty Sheila are leaving us and we all show it in our own special ways.

Dontie: moody

Me: worried

V: cross

Stanley: quiet

Anika: clingy (to Stanley)

Will: does a massive poo in his nappy

(this may have been a coincidence. He does do a lot of big poos.)

Mum: miserable

Dad: glum

Granddad: gruff

Grandma: sniffy

Uncle Vez: devastated (this means really, really sad)

We have lunch but nobody feels like eating much. Not even me.

Nobody feels like saying much either.

Afterwards, nobody feels like doing much.

'I'm going out to play,' says V defiantly. 'On my own.'

'You can't, it's starting to rain,' says Mum.

'It's not fair!' says V, but I don't think it's Mum she's cross with.

'Shall we watch a DVD instead?' suggests Aunty Sheila.

'No, we've seen them all,' says V, folding her arms.

'I could nip out and get *Paddington* for you,' offers Aunty Sheila. Stanley and Anika brighten up.

'*Paddington's* for kids,' says Dontie scornfully, even though I know he's seen it twice and loved it.

'I hate *Paddington*,' says V, which is not true.

I know how she feels though.

'Don't be rude,' says Mum automatically, though you can tell her heart's not in it. We all lapse back into miserable silence.

Gloom settles over the Butterfields like a cloud.

'I've got some work to finish off,' mumbles Dad and he slopes off to the shed (which is also his studio).

Mum sighs. 'I'd better put Will down for a nap.' Will: the only smiley face in the family.

Granddad gets to his feet. 'May as well make a move, Marjorie.'

Grandma stands up, turns to Aunty Sheila and sniffs. 'When are you off then?'

'Tomorrow,' says Aunty Sheila gently.

Uncle Vez makes a little choking noise in his throat. We all watch as he shuffles off to his room and shuts the door behind him.

My throat feels like there's a great big lump in it. Poor Uncle Vez.

He looks broken, like an old, abandoned toy.

Uncle Bruce looks stricken. He knows it's all his fault.

Grandma turns back to Aunty Sheila. 'We'll say goodbye now then,' she says coldly.

'Oh Marjorie, come here,' says Aunty Sheila and opens her arms wide for a hug. But Grandma ignores them and gives her a mean little peck on the cheek instead.

Granddad pats Uncle Bruce on the shoulder. 'Safe journey home, mate.'

Then they're gone. Without another word.

I notice something as Grandma passes me.

She wasn't being mean after all.

She's got tears streaming down her cheeks.

Like me.

Chapter 22

It was a strange afternoon.

Uncle Vez stayed shut in his room. Mum said to leave him be till he was ready to come out.

Then she disappeared upstairs with Will. I think they both went to sleep.

V rumbled and grumbled and got on everyone's nerves.

Dad was in the shed for ages. I went out to see what he was doing but he wouldn't let me in.

In the end Aunty Sheila nipped out and came back with *Paddington*, saying *she* wanted to watch it anyway.

So Stanika and I sat on the sofa and watched it with her and before long, Dontie, V, Jellico and Hiccup joined us too.

It's hard to stay miserable when you're laughing out loud. And during a sad bit, V forgot all about being cross with Aunty Sheila and snuggled up to her for a cuddle.

A little bear from Peru made things normal for a while.

But now it's nearly bedtime, and we're all back together, I remember that Aunty Sheila and Uncle Bruce are leaving in the morning and I feel really, really sad.

'I don't want you to go,' I moan. 'We'll

never see you again.'

'It's not fair!' grumbles V to Aunty Sheila. 'You never made us a pumpkin cake and you promised!'

'And you never showed me how to do CPR,' I remind her.

Aunty Sheila looks like she might cry.

'And we never got to play a return cricket match either,' says Dontie. 'The Ashes are supposed to be a series.'

'You're right mate,' says Uncle Bruce in his lovely Aussie drawl. 'We do need a return match. You're going to have to save your pennies and come over to Oz and play it sometime.'

'Can we?' I say, shooting upright in excitement.

'I wish!' says Mum, shaking her head. 'We haven't got the money to fly us all out to Australia. It would cost a fortune.'

'Ohhhh!' I sink back down again, knowing she's right. It's the other side of the world. If the Packham-Wellses couldn't afford it, then the Butterfields can't, that's for sure.

Then it dawns on me.

'But Mum!' I shout. 'We *have* got a fortune! We won the lottery, remember?'

Chapter 23

Mum's cheeks turn pink. **Oops!** I forgot! We're not supposed to tell anyone we won the lottery. It's a family secret.

But Aunty Sheila and Uncle Bruce *are* family.

V's arms shoot up in the air. 'Yaaaay!' she shrieks. 'We can come out to see you after all!'

'Hurray!' shout Stanika, bouncing up and down in excitement.

'Did you really win the lottery?' asks

Aunty Sheila, looking surprised.

Mum is embarrassed. 'Yes.'

'We won over a million pounds,' says Dontie.

'Over a million!' breathes Aunty Sheila. 'So you really could come and visit us? Oh, how wonderful that would be.'

Mum and Dad exchange guilty looks. Dad clears his throat.

'That's impossible, I'm afraid. It's all gone.'

Silence. So loud, it's deafening.

'We bought the house next door, you see,' continues Mum awkwardly. 'We knocked through, so we could stay here and Uncle Vez could come and live with us. He was all on his own.'

'That was kind of you,' says Aunty Sheila softly.

'What?' says Dontie, confused. 'Hang on a minute. I don't get it. It never cost a million pounds to knock through this house. What happened to the rest of the money?'

Mum glances uneasily at Dad. Dad glances down at the floor.

'You've spent it, haven't you?' persists Dontie.

Silence.

'THAT'S NOT FAIR!' roars V, which makes us all jump. 'Now we can't go to Australia! You've spent all the money on yourselves! You … you … you … GREEDY PIGS!'

This is the rudest thing V has ever said in her life. Immediately she flings her arms round Mum and sobs her heart out because she's sorry.

Anika sobs her heart out too because she hates shouting.

Aunty Sheila and Uncle Bruce look really uncomfortable, as if they started all this. But it's not their fault.

My mum and dad wouldn't do that, would they? Blow all the money on themselves?

What did they spend it on?

WORRY! WORRY! WORRY!

WORRY!

WORRY!

'It wasn't like that,' says Dad.

I don't know what he means.

What is happening to my lovely family?

I don't like it.

Chapter 24

'What's going on here?' says a familiar voice. 'All this blooming noise is ruining my beauty sleep!'

Uncle Vez has appeared. He's looking better now he's had a rest.

'Mum and Dad have spent all the lottery money and now we can't go to Australia,' I explain above V's sobs.

'Oh, I see,' says Uncle Vez. 'Budge up and let me sit down.'

He scoops Hiccup off the sofa and into

his lap. Hiccup runs up onto his shoulder, his favourite place, and perches there like a parrot.

Jellico comes over and nuzzles his hand and Uncle Vez gives him a scratch behind the ears.

Will grins at him and waves his rattle.

Everyone loves Uncle Vez. He slows things down. Life is always calmer when he's around.

'How do you feel about that then, Mattie love?' he asks after a while.

'Sad,' I say honestly. 'I would love to have gone out to stay with Aunty Sheila and Uncle Bruce and see Australia for myself. But I'm glad we spent it on a bigger house so you could come and live with us.'

His eyes crinkle into a smile. 'So am I.

What's our V making such a fuss about then? Don't you want me living with you, V?'

V stops sobbing and lifts her head. Her eyes are blotchy and she's very snotty, but she says in surprise, 'Of course I do!'

'It's not that,' explains Dontie. 'It's just that there should have been some left over, quite a bit actually. Enough for us all to fly out to Australia. But Mum and Dad have spent it all.'

'Oh, I see,' says Uncle Vez, nodding his head wisely and then he turns to Mum and Dad. 'And have you told them what you spent it on?'

'No!' say Mum and Dad together.

'Well, I think it's time you did.'

Uncle Vez knows!

Mum and Dad look sheepish. Or do

I mean doggish? They look like Jellico when he's done something wrong.

As if he senses it, Jellico puts his paws over his ears and whines.

'Own up. It doesn't matter what you've done, we'll still love you,' I say, which is what they always say to us when we're hiding something.

'You tell them,' says Mum, sounding about seven.

'No, you tell them,' says Dad, sounding about six.

'I'll blooming tell them, if you won't,' says Uncle Vez. 'It's time they knew.'

Mum and Dad look at each other helplessly. It must be something really, really bad.

'Who do you think saved your school for you and your friends?' asks Uncle Vez.

What's he on about?

I think back to all the things we did to make the council change their mind and keep our school open.

The committee meetings we had, right here in this room.

The protest walk we went on in the rain.

The petition we organised that Stanley handed over to our MP.

The social media campaigns.

The video we made that went viral.

The front page newspaper articles.

The television coverage.

We tried so hard but it was no good. The bottom line was, there was no money available. Nothing left to pay the teachers' wages.

Then, at the very last minute, just as

Learnwell Primary was about to close for good, somebody came to the rescue. Somebody kind and generous and wonderful. Our friend in need, our good angel, our knight in shining armour.

Nobody knows who our mystery saviour was who gave us the money we needed to keep our small village school open. We didn't even know their name. Mrs Dunnet said it was an Anonymous Benefactor.

At last the penny drops.

'It was you!' I gasp, staring at Mum and Dad open-mouthed.

'You're the Anonymous Benefactor!'

Chapter 25

I can't believe my parents did that for us. Saved our school, I mean.

V's mega-sorry she called them greedy pigs. Dontie's cool with what they did too, and he's not even at our school anymore.

It's breakfast time and we're all friends again. It's a very special breakfast because it's our last one with Aunty Sheila and Uncle Bruce.

I felt sad when I woke up but when I saw what Aunty Sheila has made for us

I cheered up.

Damper! A massive, huge pile of it.

'What's this? The last supper?' asks Uncle Vez, tucking in. He's got maple syrup in his beard.

'The last breakfast,' corrects Dontie, wolfing it down.

'It's not fair!' V is squirting syrup all over hers. 'We won't have it anymore and it's my favourite!'

'I've left the recipe for you,' says Aunty Sheila. 'You can make it yourself.'

'It won't be as good as yours,' says Stanley solemnly and Aunty Sheila ruffles his hair. Then she ruffles Anika's too so she doesn't feel left out.

I'm going to miss her so much!

'Where's Dad?' I ask to change the subject. 'He'd better hurry up or there'll be none left for him.'

'He's been out in the shed all night,' says Mum.

At that very moment Dad walks through the back door in a cloud of dust. He looks tired and red-eyed but very pleased with himself.

'All done?' asks Mum, pouring him a steaming mug of coffee.

'All done,' he replies, pinching the last piece of damper from V's plate.

'Da-ad!'

'What have you been up to?' asks Uncle Bruce.

'Take a look,' says Dad, nodding towards the window.

We jump up and peer out at the back garden.

It all looks normal.

Just the usual trees, bushes, washing line, broken bench, discarded toys, Dad's studio shed, and Uncle Vez's garden shed. Plus all the statues Dad has made for us over the years.

Automatically my eyes search out my favourite, Will's seal.

Next to him, two new statues have appeared overnight.

'Look!'' I shriek. 'Look what Dad's made!'

Everyone crowds to the window.

'A crocodile!' cries Stanley.

'And a koala!' coos Anika.

'So that's what you've been doing in the shed all this time,' chuckles Uncle Vez.

'Who are they for?' asks V, puzzled. 'It's nobody's birthday.'

'I know! I know!' I turn to Uncle Bruce

and Aunty Sheila in excitement. 'They're for you!'

'Really?'

Dad nods and Aunty Sheila's eyes shine with delight.

'Which is which?' grins Uncle Bruce.

Aunty Sheila snaps her teeth at him and everyone laughs.

'That means you're family now,' I explain.

Uncle Bruce stops grinning and blows his nose very hard.

Aunty Sheila's face crumples.

I think they're happy to be part of my funny family.

But I think they're sad they're leaving us.

Chapter 26

We all go the airport to wave goodbye to Uncle Bruce and Aunty Sheila. I'm wearing my kangaroo onesie. (Confession: I slept in it last night.) Uncle Bruce is wearing his cork hat.

It's the first time I've ever been inside an airport. It's very exciting.

People are getting ready to fly off to far-away countries and they're rushing here and there, or standing in long queues to check in.

There are shops and cafés, and banks where you can change pounds into any currency in the world, and restaurants and car-hire firms. It's like a busy city centre, only cleaner and shinier.

It's almost as good as flying. But not quite.

Uncle Bruce spends ages at one of the desks.

'I wonder if there's something wrong?' says Dad uneasily.

'Aw, no, Tim love, he's just got stuff to sort out,' says Aunty Sheila.

'I wish I was coming with you,' I say to her longingly, then glance guiltily at Mum and Dad. 'I don't mean …'

'It's OK, Mattie,' says Mum gently.

Uncle Bruce comes back from the desk with a big fat envelope in his hand.

'All right?' asks Aunty Sheila.

'All sorted,' he says, and tucks it into his inside pocket.

'Look who's here!' cries Uncle Vez. It's Grandma and Granddad charging through the airport doors towards us.

'Norman! Audrey!' Grandma flings herself into Aunty Sheila's arms. 'I'm sorry! I couldn't let you leave without saying goodbye properly!'

'Oh, Marje!' Aunty Sheila gives her a big squashy hug. 'I'm going to miss you, you cranky old goat.' We all laugh, even Grandma.

'Hush!' Dad holds his hand up and we listen to the announcement. 'Your gate is open. It's time to go through to Departures.'

Uncle Vez grabs Uncle Bruce and they

do that hugging, patting, rocking thing like they're never going to let each other go.

Then it's hugs and kisses all round, and it's all really quick, and the next second Uncle Bruce and Aunty Sheila are walking away from us.

SUDDENLY it hits me and I'm really, really sad. I'm never going to see them again.

Uncle Bruce and Aunty Sheila turn around. 'I nearly forgot,' says Uncle Bruce, and he comes back and takes the big fat envelope out of his pocket and hands it to me.

'These are for your family, Mattie. I'll leave you in charge.'

He dashes back to take his place behind Aunty Sheila who's at the front of the queue and we watch them going through security.

And then they've gone.

I look down at the envelope in my hand.

'Open it!' says Dontie, so I do.

Tickets flutter down to the floor.

'What are these?' asks Dad, as we bend down to pick them up.

'There's one for you, Anika,' I say, recognising her name. 'And Stanley. And one for Albert Trot. That's you, Uncle Vez.'

'And one for Grandma,' says Dontie. 'And Mum.'

'Is there one for me?' squeals V.

'There's one for all of us,' says Dad, scooping them up.

'What are they?' Mum grabs them and

her face lights up like a Christmas candle.

'Oh my word!' she shrieks.

'We're off to Australia!'

DEPARTURES
G9

Praise for My Funny Family

'Mattie and her family really make me laugh. Thank you for all these great books.'
– Emily-Sophie, age 5

'I love all the Funny Family books. I hope you write some more. Your books are just right for me because I like the Family and I understand them all as well. My family are quite annoying sometimes especially my older brother. Mattie I absolutely love. Once I even tried to wear a hat all the time like Mattie but it only lasted about a minute.' – Beth, age 8

'Endearing... a fun, funny slice of family life.'
– *Junior*

'Both sweet and surprising... fresh and funny. Easy to imagine this book being a turning point for independent readers.' – *Books for Keeps*

'Hilarious' – *The Guardian*

Mattie is nine years old and she worries about everything, which isn't surprising. Because when you have a family as big and crazy as hers, there's always something to worry about! Will the seeds she's planted in the garden with her brothers and sisters grow into fruit and veg like everyone promised? Why does it seem as if Grandma doesn't like them sometimes? And what's wrong with Mum?

Read the first book in the hilarious and heart-warming young series about the chaotic life of the Butterfield family.

It's the new school term and, as the baby inside Mum's tummy gets bigger and bigger, the family begins to plan for Christmas. There are lists to be made and presents to be wrapped. But could an unexpected Christmas gift be just around the corner?

Read the third book in the hilarious and heart-warming *My Funny Family* series.

www.chrishigginsthatsme.com

CHRIS HIGGINS

my Funny Family

Illustrated by Lee Wildish

CHRIS HIGGINS

My Funny Family on Holiday

CHRIS HIGGINS

My Funny Family's Got Talent

CHRIS HIGGINS

My Funny Family Gets Bigger

Illustrated by Lee Wildish

CHRIS HIGGINS

My Funny Family Moves House

Collect all the

My Funny Family

books and discover more of Mattie's adventures

Before writing her first novel, Chris Higgins taught English and Drama for many years in secondary schools and also worked at the Minack, the open-air theatre on the cliffs near Lands End. She now writes full time and is the author of nineteen books for children and teenagers.

Chris is married with four daughters. She loves to travel and has lived and worked in Australia as well as hitchhiking to Istanbul and across the Serengeti Plain. Born and brought up in South Wales, she now lives in the far west of Cornwall with her husband.